The Red Herring Fallacy
Artifice of Deception

by

Ted Cheldin

Dedicated to

The Golden Rule

PREFACE

A fallacy is a false invalid notion, a defect in an argument that involves mistaken reasoning, a misconception, a delusion. A fallacy can not be used as a legal argument as it's logic is flawed. Sometimes fallacies are committed on purpose, in order to wrongfully influence and or mislead. Repercussions of such callous dishonesty is appalling. Gone unstopped and unpunished is just as appalling. And thus it follows... such lawlessness must be relentlessly eradicated from upon the face of all the earth.

The Author
December 2023

"I will either find a way, or make one."

Hannibal, 218 BC

CONTENTS

PROLOGUE

Good morning children. Everyone calm down and take a seat. Take a seat. 17th century legal scholar Sir Edward Coke once said, *"Fraud and deceit abound in these days more than in former times."* 400 years ago children! And now, so prevalent, as ominous signs doom without restraint as history repeats itself. Today we will be discussing one of the longest running, if not the longest running, fraudulent financial schemes in history. In fact you, or someone you know, may have already fallen victim, unbeknownst to you or them, as an unwilling participant. You may experience shock, disgust, frustration, nausea, anger, helplessness, and emotional distress which may manifest itself into great physical pain. Be afraid, be very afraid, that this cruel explicit disregard for the law has gone unquelled, allowed to wildly flourish, and take root, like a giant frightening sci-fi blob. You've been warned! Hold on. You're in for a twisted convoluted ride. Let's go.

THE SCHEME

Los Angeles 2022 -

In the matter of CHELDIN V. UNITED PARCEL SERVICE (UPS), the defendant, UPS, was found liable for alleged wrongdoings and ordered to pay the plaintiff, Ted Cheldin, Compensatory and Exemplary Damages for the egregious offenses. The complaint alleged:

1) Unfair Business Practices;
2) Fraudulent Claim Denial Scheme;
3) Breach of the Implied Covenant of Good Faith and Fair Dealings;
4) Unconscionable Material Misrepresentations;
5) Breach of Contract;
6) Orchestrated a Long Running Scheme to Defraud;
7) Orchestrated a Long Running Scheme to Defraud Being Widespread, By Design, A Pattern, A Routine Practice;
8) Orchestrated a Long Running Scheme to Defraud in order to save the company money.

As alleged in the Cheldin case, the UPS scheme to defraud works like this:

1) UPS, a package delivery company, or one of their affiliates (e.g. The UPS Store), enters into a contract with a customer to ship a package, the contents of which are covered for a declared value in the event of loss or damage.

2) After entrusting UPS with a customer's package for coverage and safe delivery, a damage loss event ensues to the package contents while under their care, custody,

and control.

3) Then, after the customer files a damage loss report, and goes through a long drawn out claim process with UPS for indemnification of the damage loss event, UPS will knowingly make up, use, or cause to be made or used a false record (or records) to avoid, or decrease their obligation to pay for which they had previously agreed to in the customer's contract.

4) UPS routinely and fraudulently denies customers' claims based on the "Red Herring" fallacy in order to wrongfully influence and mislead, to reroute and distract claimants to an irrelevant invalid point, that packages/parcels were not properly packaged in accordance with their rules or guidelines published on their website, which was proven in the court case, CHELDIN V. UNITED PARCEL SERVICE, has no legal connection with the customers' contract. If a customer's package was not properly or not sufficiently packaged, UPS or their affiliate should not have entered into a contract and not accepted the customer's package. Since UPS accepts customers' packages, it follows that "sufficient" conditions are met for the contract, thus inferring packages are properly packaged, and no other "necessary" condition of "packaging" would be required in this regard. A later and unforeseen claim denial event from UPS of "Improper or Insufficient Packaging", or for any irrelevant reason, would impede any purpose for customers of entering into contracts for coverage to their parcels. At the time contracts are entered, UPS is aware of their customers' purpose and need for coverage. UPS accepts packages "as-is" thus implying that the contract

terms do not make an unforeseen event, risk of loss or damage from "Improper or Insufficient Packaging", a cause for customers' own personal loss, hardship, and something they would need to shoulder. Everyday UPS accepts, without turning away, packages and parcels wrapped in a multitude of various ways and conditions, further factually proving that a "sufficient" condition alone exists of acceptance, absent a "necessary" condition, adequate for coverage entitlement. UPS uses unconscionable material misrepresentations including the "fallacy" of "Improper or Insufficient Packaging" in a feeble attempt to escape their liability and malfeasance by shifting blame on their customers. The term "red herring" is thought to have come from long ago literary stories of training dogs and horses by use of herring fish that stink and turn red after being smoked (cooked), a deceptive ruse or trick used as a **device and artifice** to fool and distract animals from an irrelevant scent. Mystery writers such as Agatha Christe and Sir Arthur Conan Doyle made use of red herring fallacies in their story telling to twist tales, influence, and mislead readers away to invalid points of a plot.

Holy hoodwinked! That's right children. This type of business practice of fooling people is not legal, violating several state and federal laws pertaining to fraud and acts to defraud.

BUSTED

The following is a court transcript excerpt from CHELDIN V. UNITED PARCEL SERVICE:

Court Commissioner: ..."DO YOU HAVE ANY EVIDENCE WITH RESPECT TO THE ARGUMENT THAT ESSENTIALLY YOUR COMPANY IS IN BAD FAITH, IS VIOLATING THE COVENANT OF GOOD FAITH AND FAIR DEALING, AND IT ALREADY KNOWS AHEAD OF TIME THAT IT'S NOT GOING TO PAY FOR ANY DAMAGES TO THE PROPERTY? DO YOU HAVE ANY EVIDENCE -- DO YOU HAVE ANY TESTIMONY IN THAT REGARD?"...

Court Commissioner: ..."CAN YOU GIVE ME SOME KIND OF EVIDENCE THAT YOU DON'T ALWAYS JUST TAKE EVERYTHING THAT -- YOU KNOW, JUST BASICALLY DECLARE THAT EVERYTHING IS SIMPLY IMPROPERLY PACKAGED? "...

Defendant UPS: ..."I DON'T HAVE ANY EVIDENCE FOR THAT."...

Court Commissioner: ..."IS THERE ANYTHING ELSE YOU WANT TO TELL ME? YOU KNOW, I DON'T HAVE ANY EVIDENCE FROM YOU OTHER THAN THE CONTRACT HERE. IS THERE ANYTHING ELSE YOU WANT TO TELL ME?"...

Defendant UPS: ..."NO. THAT WILL BE ALL, YOUR HONOR."...

Court Commissioner: "SO I'VE RECEIVED EVIDENCE THAT ESSENTIALLY, DESPITE THIS

CLAUSE IN THE CONTRACT, THAT UPS HAS --
I'VE BEEN GIVEN EVIDENCE THAT UPS SEEMS
TO HAVE A CUSTOM AND PRACTICE OF
ESSENTIALLY DENYING ALL CLAIMS
REGARDLESS. IN THIS INSTANCE, THE
PLAINTIFF WAS ACTUALLY FORCED TO SUE UPS
JUST TO GET THE DECLARED VALUE OF THE
ITEM."

Holy foul play! That's right children. The allegations
are obviously irrefutable as the fallacy to reroute and
distract the claimants to an irrelevant invalid point (i.e.
UPS packaging rules) is published on their website, it's
Standard Operating Procedure, referenced to customers
in order to wrongfully influence or mislead, using their
claims department **employed as a device and artifice
to deceive and defraud**. The Court conclusively agreed
and resoundingly awarded exemplary damages to punish
the defendant for the wrongful acts.

THE HORROR

Holy dastardly acts! That's right children. Research conducted by Cheldin uncovered details of UPS wrongful acts going back at least 23 years (although likely much longer), **employing as a device and artifice to deceive and defraud their claims department**, and it's long-running fraudulent scheme of "Improper or Insufficient Packaging", to wrongfully deny customer package/parcel damage claims. Based on that research, estimates, analysis of public objective data from a close competitor*, the ruling in the Cheldin case, as well as the statements made in that court case, this ongoing UPS fraud affects hundreds of package damaged customers daily, and has involved an estimated $1,000,000,000 in claim money in the past 23 years alone. How much of that estimated claim money was actually paid out to UPS customers? Who's to say? However, from what has been laid bare, and brought to light in court, I dare say not much:

Court Commissioner: ..."...YOUR COMPANY...ALREADY KNOWS AHEAD OF TIME THAT IT'S NOT GOING TO PAY FOR ANY DAMAGES TO THE PROPERTY...".

Court Commissioner: ..."UPS SEEMS TO HAVE A CUSTOM AND PRACTICE OF ESSENTIALLY DENYING ALL CLAIMS REGARDLESS...".

For the fiscal years 2018-2020, The United States Postal Service (USPS), a close UPS competitor, reported $121,301,181 adjudicated indemnity claims to the Office of the Inspector General. For comparison, those USPS figures average out to $929,975,721 extrapolated over 23 years, or approximately $1,000,000,000.

Holy Cow! Did you say a Billion Dollars? That's right children. However likely much more. These estimates are based on domestic US figures for the past 23 years and therefore including worldwide claims and more years would equate to much more than a billion dollars. It's an underhanded scheme of epic proportion.

Holy treachery! That's right children. And that's not all. Like birds of a feather, other package delivery companies may have crossed over to the dark side as well when it comes to processing package damage claims in the same manner. If so, they've been laughing all the way to the bank with your claim money (i.e. ill-gotten gains). It's disgustingly scandalous!

GO DIRECTLY TO PRISON

Holy bad faith! That's right children. It's despicably horrific! And not only that, it appears the game's afoot, and here's why. Such acts are not only fraudulent, but mislead others about revenue sources retained from ill-gotten gains derived from money belonging to others (e.g. claims customers), which artificially inflate financial figures in reports to shareholders, investors, and the Securities & Exchange Commission (SEC). You see children, by making these sorts of material misrepresentations of ill-gotten gains on corporate books, accountants can help increase the net income from the core business operations. This diversion of funds from ill-gotten gains reported incorrectly creates a misappropriation of income where the effect causes the financial statements not to be presented, in all material aspects, in conformity with Generally Accepted Accounting Principles (GAAP). This is harmful to financial statement users (e.g. investors) in order to correctly assess the direct business activities on the income statement of the company. This harms its own employees, customers, investors, and the government who will look for honest transparency in a business operation, accounting, and SEC reporting. It's so damn unscrupulous!

Holy cooked books! That's right children. For your homework assignment tonight, please study violations of SEC Rule 17(a) and SEC Rule 10b-5 and thereunder. And for extra credit, study Department of Justice (DOJ) Criminal Resource Manual (CRM) section 942. You will be tested soon, and your answers will go on your permanent record.

FOR SHAME, FOR SHAME

Holy shenanigans! That's right children. Something smells repulsively rotten. Where have the checks and balances been hiding? In this regard, package delivery company auditors and accountants as co-conspirators, aiding and abetting, may be culpable as well. It is understood that the general standard of auditor independence under the requirements of the SEC, Office of the Chief Accountant, is that an auditor is not independent with respect to the audit client if a reasonable, fully informed investor would conclude that the auditor is not capable of exercising objective and impartial judgment on all issues encompassed within the audit engagement. Therefore, it's a telltale sign that if such auditor independence had been in place, it would have surely detected such accounting deficiencies and wrongdoings as stated above. A child of age 5 would understand this stuff. If you're a child of at least age 5, please raise your hand.

Holy bamboozled! That's right children. And let's not forget, package delivery company customers include numerous branches of city, county, state, federal governments, and government military contractors. It may likely be that their package damage claims are denied in the same illegal manner. A scheme to defraud can con thousands, including consumers, investors, and even government law enforcement officials. If you enjoy being made a fool of, please raise your hand. Anyone? Anyone?

HELP!

Holy pull the wool over one's eyes! That's right children. If it walks like a duck, it talks like a duck, it's most likely a damn duck! Although granted, it could also be a damn wolf in sheep's clothing. Yup, you've all been duped!

Holy matter of public interest! That's right children. The only thing necessary for evil to triumph is for good men [and women] to do nothing. To assist victims, and those who continue to suffer from such ongoing fraud, help was requested from the following elected officials and, to the best of my knowledge, have done nothing:

Republican Congressman Mike Garcia, notified December 20, 2022, and did nothing;

Democratic Vice President Kamala Harris, notified December 21, 2022, and did nothing;

Democratic Senator Dianne Feinstein, notified January 12, 2023, and did nothing;

Republican Assemblyman Tom Lackey, notified January 19, 2023, and did nothing;

Republican Senator Scott Wilk, notified March 6, 2023, and did nothing.

Holy remiss nonfeasance in office! That's right children. Since those empowered to do something in your best interest, have chosen to sit on their proverbial laurels and do nothing, make your voice heard! Do not vote for politicians that make hollow promises of being tough on fraud! Exercise your rights, especially as a victim of fraud. Do the right thing! If you have fallen victim to a similar fraudulent act as explained herein, know someone that has, or happen to be employed by such wrongdoers, tips, reports, complaints, and or help with retribution may be filed with the proper authorities online, by regular mail, or by phone (see contact info below).

United States Securities & Exchange Commission (SEC):

Website: sec.gov/whistleblower

Mail: SEC Office of the Whistleblower (c/o ENF-CPU)
        14420 Albemarle Point Place
        Suite 102
        Chantilly, VA 20151-1750

Phone: (202) 551-4790
Fax: (703) 813-9322

United States Department of Justice (DOJ):

Website: fbi.gov/investigate/white-collar-crime

Mail: FBI Headquarters
        935 Pennsylvania Avenue, NW
        Washington, D.C. 20535-0001

Phone: (202) 324-3000

EPILOGUE

Holy hornswoggled! That's right children. You've all been snookered, double-crossed, and cheated! If you enjoy culprits taking advantage of you, deceiving you, stealing your hard earned money, then hell, go back to bed. I don't know about you, but if someone messes with me, I take care of business! Govern yourself accordingly. Class dismissed.

Ted Cheldin is the author of, *Fundamentally Crazy*, available at Amazon.com and other book sellers. Mr. Cheldin can be reached at: tedcheldin@hotmail.com.

APPENDIX

1

1   IN THE SUPERIOR COURT OF THE STATE OF CALIFORNIA

2   FOR THE COUNTY OF LOS ANGELES

3   DEPARTMENT A22   HON. MARCELO D'ASERO

4

5   TED CHELDIN,   )
)
6   PLAINTIFF,   )
    VS.   )
7   )   CASE NO. 22AVSC00096
    UNITED PARCEL SERVICE, INC.,)
8   )
                    DEFENDANT.   )
9   _____)

10   TRANSCRIPT OF PROCEEDINGS

11   NON-JURY TRIAL

12

13   APRIL 12, 2022

14 **APPEARANCES**

15
    FOR THE PLAINTIFF: IN PROPRIA PERSONA
16

17 FOR THE DEFENDANT: FELIPE AVITIA
18   UNITED PARCEL SERVICE, INC.
                              55 GLENLAKE PARKWAY NE
19   ATLANTA, GA 30328

20

21

22

23

24

25

26 PROCEEDINGS RECORDED BY ELECTRONIC SOUND RECORDING; TRANSCRIPT
    PRODUCED BY ESCRIBERS, LLC
27

28

e)cribers
www.escribers.net | 800-257-0885

1   I N D E X

2

6

7

8

9

10

11

12

13

14

15

16

17

18

19

20

21

22

23

24

25

26

27

28

```
 1  CASE NUMBER:        22AVSC00096
 2  CASE NAME:          TED CHELDIN VS. UNITED PARCEL SERVICE,
 3                      INC.
 4  LANCASTER, CA       TUESDAY, APRIL 12, 2022
 5  DEPARTMENT A22      HON. MARCELO D'ASERO, JUDGE
 6  TRANSCRIBER:        COLE TUTINO
 7  TIME:               A.M. SESSION
 8  APPEARANCES:
 9              THE DEFENDANT PRESENT REPRESENTED BY FELIPE AVITIA;
10              THE PLAINTIFF PRESENT APPEARING IN PROPRIA PERSONA.
11
12              THE COURT:  ALL RIGHT.  THE COURT CALLS THE MATTER
13  OF TED CHELDIN -- OR [SHEL'-DON] V. UNITED PARCEL SERVICE,
14  INC., CASE NUMBER 22AVSC00096.  THIS MATTER IS HERE FOR SMALL
15  CLAIMS NON-JURY TRIAL.  DO I HAVE TED CHELDIN HERE?
16              MR. CHELDIN:  YES, YOUR HONOR.
17              THE COURT:  IS THAT CORRECT, THE WAY I PRONOUNCED
18  YOUR NAME?
19              MR. CHELDIN:  [SHEL'-DON].  YES, YOUR HONOR.
20              THE COURT:  OKAY.  AND PLEASE -- THE UNITED PARCEL
21  SERVICE INDIVIDUAL, PLEASE GIVE YOUR APPEARANCE AGAIN.
22              MR. AVITIA:  FELIPE AVITIA.
23              THE COURT:  OKAY.
24              THE CLERK:  WE NEED A -- I GUESS VERBAL
25  AUTHORIZATION.
26              THE COURT:  RIGHT.  LET ME JUST SWEAR EVERYBODY IN,
27  AND THEN I'LL ASK YOU WHETHER YOU'RE AUTHORIZED.
28              SO JOHN, WOULD YOU DO US THE FAVOR, PLEASE?
```

1   THE CLERK: AND WOULD YOU PLEASE STAND AND RAISE

2 YOUR RIGHT HAND, AND LET ME KNOW WHEN YOU'VE DONE SO?

3   MR. AVITIA: OKAY.

4   THE COURT: ALL RIGHT. DO YOU AND EACH OF YOU

5 SOLEMNLY STATE THAT THE TESTIMONY YOU MAY GIVE IN THE CAUSE

6 NOW PENDING BEFORE THIS COURT SHALL BE THE TRUTH, THE WHOLE

7 TRUTH, AND NOTHING BUT THE TRUTH, SO HELP YOU GOD?

8   MR. CHELDIN: I DO.

9   MR. AVITIA: YES.

10   THE COURT: OKAY. ALL RIGHT. REAL QUICKLY, I HAVE

11 MR. CHELDIN'S EVIDENCE HERE. I DON'T HAVE ANY EVIDENCE FROM

12 UNITED PARCEL. IS THERE A REASON FOR THAT, SIR?

13   MR. AVITIA: YES. SO WE HAD ATTEMPTED TO SETTLE,

14 AND FOR THE MOST PART, IF WE NEEDED TO REFERENCE ANY OF OUR,

15 LIKE, EVIDENCE, IT WOULD BE THROUGH OUR TERMS AND CONDITIONS

16 THAT ARE ACKNOWLEDGED AND SUBMITTED BY MR. CHELDIN.

17   THE COURT: OKAY. I'VE LOST YOU. ARE YOU SAYING

18 THAT YOU'RE GOING TO RELY ON MR. CHELDIN'S EVIDENCE?

19   MR. AVITIA: YES.

20   THE COURT: OKAY. I JUST NEED TO ASK, ARE YOU

21 AUTHORIZED TO APPEAR ON BEHALF OF UNITED PARCEL?

22   MR. AVITIA: YES, I AM.

23   THE COURT: ALL RIGHT. WHAT'S YOUR RELATIONSHIP TO

24 THIS CASE? DO YOU HAVE ANY PERSONAL KNOWLEDGE OF MR.

25 CHELDIN'S ACCOUNT WITH UNITED PARCEL, OR ARE YOU JUST A

26 FUNCTIONARY, IF YOU'LL FORGIVE ME?

27   MR. AVITIA: YEAH. I WAS -- I WAS ASSIGNED WITH THE

28 CASE, AND I HAVE THE EVIDENCE IN FRONT OF (AUDIO

1   INTERFERENCE).

2   THE COURT: OKAY. ALL RIGHT, LET ME LOOK AT THE

3   COMPLAINT REAL QUICKLY. ALL RIGHT. MR. CHELDIN IS SUING

4   FOR -- LET ME MAKE SURE I'M LOOKING AT THE RIGHT -- YES. ALL

5   RIGHT. MR. CHELDIN IS LOOKING AT SUING FOR $4,700 FOR BREACH

6   OF CONTRACT, BREACH OF IMPLIED COVENANT OF GOOD FAITH, UNFAIR

7   DEALING, UNFAIR BUSINESS PRACTICES, FRAUD, EMOTIONAL DISTRESS,

8   COMPENSATORY DAMAGE DONE.

9   NOW, MR. CHELDIN, I'M GOING TO TELL YOU RIGHT NOW,

10   EMOTIONAL DISTRESS -- PUNITIVE DAMAGES ARE GOING TO BE DARN

11   NEAR IMPOSSIBLE TO SHOW UNLESS YOU CAN GIVE ME SOME SORT OF --

12   UNLESS YOU CAN GIVE ME BASICALLY WHAT THE NET WORTH OF THE

13   COMPANY IS AND HOW MUCH I WOULD HAVE TO -- YOU KNOW, BUT

14   HONESTLY, I'M NOT SURE I CAN GIVE YOU THAT. LET ME JUST ASK,

15   HOW IS IT THAT YOU BELIEVE THAT YOU'RE OWED $4,700?

16   MR. CHELDIN: THE $200 IN COMPENSATORY DAMAGES UNDER

17   MY DECLARATION, THERE'S $1,000 FOR THE FRAUD THAT I'LL EXPLAIN

18   TO THE COURT. THEY HAVE CONCOCTED A LONG-RUNNING PRACTICE TO

19   DECEIVE CUSTOMERS THAT COME IN AND MAIL PACKAGES, WHICH I'LL

20   PROVE TO THE COURT BY LOGIC AND BY THE LAW. AND EXEMPLARY

21   DAMAGES, $3,500.

22   THE COURT: OKAY. HOW DID YOU COME UP WITH $3,500?

23   MR. CHELDIN: NOMINAL AMOUNT BASED ON THE

24   COMPENSATORY DAMAGES.

25   THE COURT: OKAY. SO YOU USED A MULTIPLIER OF SOME

26   SORT?

27   MR. CHELDIN: I -- I DID. FIVE TIMES THE

28   COMPENSATORY DAMAGES, A MINIMAL AMOUNT. I KNOW PEOPLE COME IN

1 AND ASK FOR THE MAXIMUM OF 10,000. I'M NOT DOING THAT. I --
2 IF YOU WANT TO ADJUST THE AMOUNT IF YOU FIND IN MY FAVOR, YOUR
3 HONOR, THAT I'VE PROVEN MY CASE, PLEASE FEEL FREE. IT'S --
4 IT'S --
5   THE COURT: OKAY. BECAUSE REMEMBER --
6   MR. CHELDIN: I FEEL -- I FEEL --
7   THE COURT: -- FRAUD IS -- YOU KNOW, WHAT IS IT?
8 THE FIVE FINGERS OF FRAUD, RIGHT? YOU'VE GOT TO HAVE SOME
9 SORT OF REPRESENTATION IT WAS INTENDED TO BASICALLY DECEIVE
10 YOU, AND YOU HAD -- THEY CAUSED YOU TO HAVE DAMAGES. YOU
11 UNDERSTAND? SO --
12   MR. CHELDIN: AND I RELIED ON --
13   THE COURT: -- YOU NEED TO --
14   MR. CHELDIN: -- I RELIED --
15   THE COURT: -- YOU'RE GOING TO NEED TO SHOW THAT
16 THIS -- I MEAN, THIS IS A -- IF I'M NOT MISTAKEN, IT'S UPS,
17 RIGHT?
18   MR. CHELDIN: THAT'S CORRECT, YOUR HONOR.
19   THE COURT: OKAY.
20   MR. CHELDIN: YES.
21   THE COURT: SO THIS IS A NATIONAL, POSSIBLY EVEN
22 INTERNATIONAL CORPORATION --
23   MR. CHELDIN: MULTINATIONAL.
24   THE COURT: -- RIGHT? OKAY.
25   MR. CHELDIN: MULTINATIONAL.
26   THE COURT: OKAY. SO I'M JUST TELLING YOU RIGHT OFF
27 THE BAT, IT DOESN'T SEEM TO ME, UNLESS -- I MEAN, I DON'T KNOW
28 WHAT YOUR EVIDENCE IS GOING TO SHOW, BUT IT DOESN'T SEEM TO ME

1 TO BE ENTIRELY CREDIBLE THAT A MULTINATIONAL CORPORATION IS

2 GOING TO HAVE BUSINESS PRACTICES THAT ARE GOING TO BE

3 INTRINSICALLY FRAUDULENT, ALL RIGHT? NOBODY COULD DO BUSINESS

4 FOR VERY LONG DOING THAT SORT OF THING. SO, I MEAN, YOUR

5 EVIDENCE BETTER BE VERY GOOD, OKAY?

6   MR. CHELDIN: I FEEL IT IS, YOUR HONOR.

7   THE COURT: OKAY. SO WITH RESPECT TO OUT-OF-POCKET,

8 CAN YOU JUST GIVE ME AN IDEA, WHAT IS YOUR OUT-OF-POCKET

9 DAMAGES?

10   MR. CHELDIN: SURE. THE COURT COSTS, THE SERVICE

11 COSTS --

12   THE COURT: NO, THOSE ARE YOUR COSTS. I WANT YOUR

13 OUT-OF-POCKET DAMAGES.

14   MR. CHELDIN: THE $200 FOR THE ITEM THAT WAS

15 DESTROYED BY THEIR DRIVER.

16   THE COURT: OKAY. LET ME JUST ASK, SIR, THE

17 REPRESENTATIVE OF UNITED PARCEL, WHAT IS IT THAT YOU WERE

18 GOING TO -- HOW MUCH WERE YOU GOING TO OFFER IN COMPENSATION?

19   MR. AVITIA: THE $200 ON THE DECLARED VALUE AND THE

20 TOTAL SHIPPING COSTS OF $17.75, FOR A TOTAL OF $217.75.

21   THE COURT: OKAY. ALL RIGHT. THAT'S THE OFFER, AND

22 YOU'VE REJECTED IT OUTRIGHT?

23   MR. CHELDIN: NO, THAT WAS -- THAT'S NOT THE CASE,

24 YOUR HONOR.

25   THE COURT: YOU HAVE NOT --

26   MR. CHELDIN: WHAT --

27   THE COURT: -- REJECTED IT OUTRIGHT?

28   MR. CHELDIN: WHAT HAPPENED IS I GOT A CALL ON MARCH

1 29TH FROM A FELIPE REPRESENTING HIMSELF AS SOMEONE ON BEHALF
2 OF UPS. HE WAS REACHING OUT TO ME AS -- HE LEFT A VOICE
3 MESSAGE FIRST, SAYING HE'S REACHING OUT TO ME TO SEE IF WE
4 COULD COME TO A SETTLEMENT. I CALLED HIM BACK ABOUT AN HOUR
5 LATER. I SPOKE TO HIM. I SAID -- HE REITERATED THE SAME
6 THING. I SAID, I HAVE FILED ACCORDING TO WHAT THE COURT GAVE
7 ME, THE ONLINE DISPUTE RESOLUTION FORMS, WHICH THE SHERIFF HAS
8 SERVED ON YOU. AND FEEL FREE TO MAKE AN OFFER THROUGH THAT,
9 AND I'LL LOOK AT IT.
10   AND HE SAID -- FELIPE SAID HE WAS NOT FAMILIAR WITH
11 THAT. AND I SAID, GO TO -- I THINK IT'S CALLED TURBOCOURT.COM
12 OR .ORG AND PUT IN THE CASE NUMBER I'VE REGISTERED. AND I'VE
13 ALREADY PUT IN MY AMOUNT, WHICH IS -- WHICH IS BEFORE THE
14 COURT HERE TODAY, WHICH I FEEL I'M ENTITLED TO. AND HE SAID,
15 OKAY. AND I SAID, IF -- IF SOMETHING CAN'T BE DONE THAT WAY,
16 I'LL SEE YOU ON THE COURT DATE. AND HE SAID, OKAY. AND THAT
17 WAS THE END OF THE CONVERSATION IN ITS ENTIRETY.
18   THE COURT: THE SUM OF $217.75, IS THAT ACCEPTABLE
19 OR UNACCEPTABLE TO YOU?
20   MR. CHELDIN: UNACCEPTABLE.
21   THE COURT: OKAY. THAT'S REALLY ALL I WANTED TO GET
22 TO, OKAY? SO LET ME -- ALL RIGHT. SO MY SHORT-TERM MEMORY IS
23 WORKING, RIGHT? EVERYBODY WAS SWORN IN?
24   THE CLERK: YES, YOUR HONOR.
25   THE COURT: THANK YOU.
26   OKAY, SIR, SO I'M LOOKING AT YOUR EXHIBITS. YOU'VE
27 BEEN SWORN IN. I SEE THE FIRST EXHIBIT THAT'S OF ANY
28 RELEVANCE IS EXHIBIT NUMBER 1, AND IT'S YOUR PARCEL SHIPPING

1 ORDER TERMS AND CONDITIONS. IT SHOWS DECLARED VALUE OF AN

2 ITEM BEING SENT TO AN INDIVIDUAL IN GLENDORA, ALL RIGHT, FOR

3 $200, CORRECT? IS THERE ANYTHING I SHOULD INFER FROM EXHIBIT

4 NUMBER 1 OTHER THAN WHAT I'VE JUST GOTTEN? IS THERE ANYTHING

5 YOU WANT ME TO INFER FROM THIS EXHIBIT?

6   MR. CHELDIN: YES, YOUR HONOR, THAT CONTRACT WAS --

7 WAS -- IN THE CONDITIONS, IT WAS IMPLIED THAT THIS WAS

8 SUFFICIENT ENOUGH FOR A BINDING CONTRACT AND THAT IF ANYTHING

9 HAPPENED TO THE ITEM, THAT THAT $200 WOULD -- IF ANYTHING

10 HAPPENED AFTER IT WAS IN THE CARE AND CUSTODY OF UPS, THE $200

11 WOULD BE PAID.

12   THE COURT: DO YOU WANT TO DRAW MY ATTENTION OR

13 DIRECT MY ATTENTION TO WHERE THE CONTRACT SAYS THIS? DO YOU

14 HAVE YOUR OWN COPY?

15   MR. CHELDIN: UPPER RIGHT CORNER. DECLARED VALUE,

16 $200.

17   THE COURT: RIGHT. WELL, THAT'S THE DECLARED VALUE,

18 BUT WHERE'S THE TERMS OF THE CONTRACT THAT SAY WHAT YOU WERE

19 TELLING ME IT SAYS? I DON'T DISBELIEVE THAT IT SAYS THAT; I

20 JUST NEED TO -- I JUST NEED TO SEE REAL QUICK. IT SAYS

21 HERE --

22   MR. CHELDIN: WHAT --

23   THE COURT: IF WE GO DOWN ONE, TWO, THREE, FOUR,

24 FIVE, SIX PARAGRAPHS, WE SEE,

25   "ANY STATEMENT BY U.S. REGARDING -- US,

26   (INDISCERNIBLE) ONLY AN ESTIMATE, NOT WARRANTING --

27   WE ARE NOT LIABLE FOR ANY CONSEQUENTIAL, INDIRECT,

28   SPECIAL, INCIDENTAL, OR PUNITIVE DAMAGES, OR ANY

1   LOSS OR DAMAGE RESULTING FROM DELAYS IN SHIPPING OR

2   DELIVERY."

3   SO WHAT ENDED UP HAPPENING? DID THE RECIPIENT IN

4   GLENDORA NEVER RECEIVE THE PACKAGE?

5   MR. CHELDIN: NO, THEY RECEIVED IT; IT WAS JUST

6   DESTROYED IN TRANSIT. YOU KNOW, FOR -- FOR -- THEIR DENIAL --

7   THE COURT: BUT SEE, THEY'RE ONLY DENYING FOR

8   DELAYS. THEY'RE NOT -- OKAY, WHERE DOES IT SAY THAT -- WHERE

9   DOES IT SAY THAT THEY'LL BE RESPONSIBLE? IS THAT THE DECLARED

10   VALUE PROGRAM --

11   MR. CHELDIN: THERE --

12   THE COURT: -- PARAGRAPH?

13   MR. CHELDIN: THERE IT IS. OKAY.

14   THE COURT: "UPS OFFERS A DECLARED VALUE PROGRAM

15   PROVIDING DECLARED VALUE LIMITS FOR LOSS AND DAMAGE.

16   THE DECLARED VALUE WILL BE AVAILABLE ONLY IF YOU

17   COMPLY WITH ALL TERMS AND CONDITIONS. WE SURCHARGE

18   THE COST OF THIS PRODUCT IF YOU ELECT TO

19   PARTICIPATE. WE WILL DECLARE VALUE", ET CETERA.

20   "YOU EXPRESSLY ACKNOWLEDGE THAT THE VALUE OF EACH

21   PROCESS" -- AND I SEE THE AMOUNT YOU LIST. "IF YOU

22   DO NOT DECLARE A VALUE ABOVE $100 AND PAY AN

23   ADDITIONAL CHARGE FOR" -- "YOU WILL NOT BE ENTITLED

24   TO RECOVER MORE THAN $100. THE CARRIER TERMS AND

25   CONDITIONS" --

26   OKAY. IT LOOKS LIKE YOU'RE COMPLIANT.

27   MR. CHELDIN: THANK YOU, YOUR HONOR.

28   THE COURT: RIGHT? IT LOOKS LIKE -- WELL, WAIT A

1 MINUTE. HANG ON. LET ME ASK YOU, DID YOU COMPLY WITH THEIR

2 DECLARED VALUE PROGRAM?

3   MR. CHELDIN: YES, YOUR HONOR.

4   THE COURT: OKAY. RESEARCH -- "IF YOU ELECT TO

5 PARTICIPATE IN THE DECLARED" -- OKAY. OKAY. ALL RIGHT.

6   MR. CHELDIN: AND A SEPARATE -- THEY ONLY COVER IT

7 FOR $100 UNLESS YOU PAY A SEPARATE CHARGE FOR --

8   THE COURT: RIGHT. I SEE THAT.

9   MR. CHELDIN: YEAH.

10   THE COURT: I SEE THAT. OKAY.

11   MR. CHELDIN: SO THAT'S -- THAT'S THE PROGRAM.

12   THE COURT: OKAY. ALL RIGHT.

13   MR. CHELDIN: SO I PAID -- I PAID MORE, THE $200.

14   THE COURT: OKAY. SO WE'VE GOT THAT. SERVICE

15 OPTIONS. IN THE INVOICE, IT SAYS, "GROUND RESIDENTIAL,

16 $15.03. SERVICE OPTIONS, 250". WHAT WAS THAT FOR?

17   MR. CHELDIN: THAT -- THAT'S THE -- THE COST TO --

18 TO --

19   THE COURT: OKAY.

20   MR. CHELDIN: -- MAIL -- MAIL THIS STUFF -- MAIL

21 THE --

22   THE COURT: ALL RIGHT.

23   MR. CHELDIN: -- MAIL THE PACKAGE. ACTUALLY, TWO

24 ITEMS WERE DONE AT THAT DATE --

25   THE COURT: OKAY. AND --

26   MR. CHELDIN: -- WERE SENT. THIS IS THE ONE THAT

27 GOT DESTROYED.

28   THE COURT: OKAY, THE $15.70 ONE? BECAUSE YOU PAID

1 FOR A $16.86?

2   MR. CHELDIN: YEAH. YES, SIR.

3   THE COURT: OKAY.

4   MR. CHELDIN: YES, SIR.

5   THE COURT: OKAY. AND I SEE IT. ALL RIGHT. SO

6 LET'S GO TO -- LET'S GO TO EXHIBIT NUMBER 2.

7   MR. CHELDIN: EXHIBIT 2 IS THE CLAIM INFORMATION.

8 AFTER -- IN THE BACK OF EXHIBIT 2 IS ALL THE PICTURES OF THE

9 PACKAGE WHEN IT WAS RECEIVED AT THE CUSTOMER.

10   THE COURT: OKAY.

11   MR. CHELDIN: AND YOU CAN SEE IT'S CLEARLY BROKEN.

12 SHE HAD THE PRESENCE OF MIND TO TAKE PICTURES OF IT BEFORE AND

13 AFTER IT WAS UNWRAPPED BECAUSE SHE HEARD THE SHATTERING OF THE

14 GLASS.

15   THE COURT: OKAY. SO I SEE THERE'S SOME SORT OF --

16 SOME SORT OF LETTER -- I MEAN -- YEAH, LETTER-SIZE -- NOT

17 LETTER, LIKE A SMALL LETTER, BUT EIGHT-AND-A-HALF BY ELEVEN-

18 INCH LETTER-SIZED PACKAGE. IT SAYS EBAY ON IT, "PLEASE HANDLE

19 WITH CARE".

20   MR. CHELDIN: OH, OH, IT'S -- IT'S BIG. IT'S A

21 FRAMED PICTURE --

22   THE COURT: OH, OKAY.

23   MR. CHELDIN: -- YOUR HONOR.

24   THE COURT: OKAY, IT SAYS, "FRAGILE".

25   MR. CHELDIN: YEAH.

26   THE COURT: "PLEASE HANDLE WITH CARE". I SEE IT'S

27 22 INCHES LONG.

28   MR. CHELDIN: THERE SHOULD BE COPIES OF THE PICTURE,

1 TOO.

2   THE COURT: YEAH. FOUR INCHES --

3   MR. CHELDIN: LET ME SEE WHERE THE PICTURE IS.

4   THE COURT: -- IN THICKNESS, IT LOOKS LIKE. OKAY.

5 AND 28 INCHES IN THE OTHER -- I GUESS 26 INCHES LONG, 22

6 INCHES WIDE. OKAY. AND THE OTHER SIDE OF THE BOX. SIDE OF

7 THE BOX. AND THEN SHE -- THERE'S PICTURES OF IT OPENED UP,

8 AND THEN THERE IT IS IN SOME SORT OF BLACK WRAPPING, AND IT

9 LOOKS LIKE THE GLASS IS SHATTERED. OKAY.

10   MR. CHELDIN: YEAH. THE -- THE CORRESPONDENCE IS

11 THE CLAIM INFORMATION GOING BACK AND FORTH WITH THE UPS STORE

12 AND THE UPS CLAIMS DEPARTMENT, AND --

13   THE COURT: OKAY.

14   MR. CHELDIN: -- INEVITABLY -- INEVITABLY, THEIR

15 DENIAL ON THE -- ON THE CLAIM FOR --

16   THE COURT: OKAY. SO THERE'S THE SHATTERED GLASS ON

17 THE PICTURE. I SEE MORE OF THOSE. MORE SHATTERED GLASS.

18 REALLY, I DON'T SEE ANYTHING WRONG WITH THE FRAME ITSELF. WAS

19 THERE ANYTHING WRONG WITH THE FRAME, OTHER THAN THE GLASS

20 SHATTER?

21   MR. CHELDIN: OH -- OH, THE -- WELL, THE -- THE

22 OUTSIDE OF THE FRAME IS METAL. THE GLASS IS SHATTERED. THE

23 JAGGED ITEMS DESTROYED THE ARTWORK.

24   THE COURT: OH, I SEE. THEY DESTROYED THE ARTWORK.

25   MR. CHELDIN: IT WAS BY LUKE EASTMAN. YEAH, IT'S

26 RIGHT -- I MEAN, IT'S RIGHT HERE. YOU CAN SEE THE

27 SHATTERED -- IT'S -- IT SCRATCHED IT.

28   THE COURT: YEAH, I SEE THE SCRATCHES.

1   MR. CHELDIN: YEAH.

2   THE COURT: OKAY. ALL RIGHT.

3   MR. CHELDIN: IT WAS -- IT'S RENDERED WORTHLESS.

4   THE COURT: OKAY. ALL RIGHT.

5   MR. CHELDIN: SO --

6   THE COURT: ALL RIGHT. SO NOW, I'M STILL IN EXHIBIT

7   NUMBER 2.

8   MR. CHELDIN: YES, SIR.

9   THE COURT: I WENT TO THE BACK TO LOOK AT THE -- TO

10   LOOK AT THE PICTURES. I SEE WHAT LOOKS LIKE A WEBPAGE TO

11   BASICALLY, I GUESS, REPORT YOUR DAMAGE, CORRECT?

12   MR. CHELDIN: THIS IS CORRESPONDENCE BETWEEN ME AND

13   THE UPS STORE AND ME AND THE -- THE COMPANY THAT'S HANDLING

14   THE --

15   THE COURT: OKAY. WELL, THAT'S NEXT AFTER THE

16   WEBPAGE, A PHOTOCOPY PRINTOUT OF THE WEBPAGE. AND IT SAYS

17   HERE,

18   "DEAR UPS CLAIMS DEPARTMENT, THE ATTACHED SIX PHOTO

19   DOCUMENTS SHOULD BE SUFFICIENT TO PROCESS AND PAY

20   THIS CLAIM PROMPTLY. I'M NOT GOING TO HAVE THE

21   CUSTOMER SHOVE THE ARTWORK YOUR DRIVER DESTROYED

22   ALONG WITH PIECES OF SHARP" --

23   MR. CHELDIN: THAT'S WHAT THEY WANTED US -- ME TO

24   DO.

25   THE COURT: "IN FACT, I DON'T EVEN WANT HER TO GO

26   NEAR THE BOX, OR SHE MAY LIKELY GET INJURED FROM ALL

27   THE SHARP, JAGGED, BROKEN GLASS. SHE TOLD ME SHE

28   WOULD HOLD ON TO ALL THE MATERIAL IF YOU'D LIKE TO

1   INSPECT IT. IT WOULD BE" -- "I'M WAITING TO GET
2   PAID FROM YOU," ET CETERA.
3   MR. CHELDIN: YES, SIR.
4   THE COURT: OKAY. AND THEN YOU SENT THAT? IT'S
5   YOUR TESTIMONY --
6   MR. CHELDIN: YES, SIR.
7   THE COURT: -- THIS MORNING YOU SENT -- THIS LETTER
8   WAS SENT TO THE UPS FOLKS?
9   MR. CHELDIN: YES, SIR.
10   THE COURT: OKAY.
11   MR. CHELDIN: BOTH THE UPS STORE AND THE CLAIMS
12 PERSON.
13   THE COURT: OKAY. AND THEN THEY WRITE BACK TO
14 YOU -- IT LOOKS LIKE YOU GAVE ME A PHOTOCOPY OF WHAT LOOKS
15 LIKE AN EMAIL FROM UPS PICTURES.
16   "DEAR CHELDIN, I'M TRULY SORRY THE PACKAGE WAS
17   DELIVERED DAMAGED. I WANT TO THANK YOU FOR THE
18   PHOTOS YOU HAVE SENT FOR INSPECTION. UNFORTUNATELY,
19   WE STILL NEED ADDITIONAL PICTURES. WE NEED THE
20   FOLLOWING"
21   AND THEY WANTED PHOTOS. PHOTO, PHOTO, PHOTO, PHOTO.
22   "WE WILL BE EXPECTING THIS PHOTO TO PROCEED WITH
23   PROCESSING THE CLAIM." OKAY.
24   MR. CHELDIN: SO THEN I HAD HER -- HAVE -- HAD TO GO
25 BACK AND ASK HER FOR MORE PHOTOS WITH -- TO -- JUST TO COMPLY,
26 WHICH I THOUGHT WAS LUDICROUS TO --
27   THE COURT: OKAY.
28   MR. CHELDIN: -- BEGIN WITH. SO I KNEW AT THIS

1   POINT -- BECAUSE I'VE BEEN IN THE INSURANCE BUSINESS ALL MY

2   LIFE -- THAT THEY WERE DRAGGING THEIR FEET FOR -- FOR LEADING

3   UP TO A POTENTIAL DENIAL FOR -- FOR WHO KNOWS WHAT REASON.

4   THE COURT: OKAY. OKAY, ALL RIGHT. BUT LET'S GET

5   THERE. LET'S --

6   MR. CHELDIN: YES, SIR.

7   THE COURT: -- LET THE EVIDENCE --

8   MR. CHELDIN: YES, SIR.

9   THE COURT: -- SHOW THAT. OKAY?

10   MR. CHELDIN: OF COURSE.

11   THE COURT: ALL RIGHT. SO,

12   "MR. CHELDIN, FIRST OF ALL, LET ME OFFER MY

13   APOLOGIES. NOT ONLY IS IT A MATERIAL LOSS, IT ALSO

14   RESULTED", BLAH, BLAH BLAH. "I WILL BE FORWARDING

15   THESE PHOTOS TO THE CLAIMS DEPARTMENT. THE CLAIMS

16   DEPARTMENT DOES FUNCTION AS AN INDEPENDENT

17   ARBITRATOR. SHOULD THIS ADDITIONAL EVIDENCE FAIL TO

18   SWAY THEIR FINAL JUDGMENT, I'LL REFUND YOU $17.75

19   YOU WERE CHARGED FOR THE INITIAL SHIPMENT."

20   OKAY.

21   MR. CHELDIN: YEAH, THAT'S AARON (PHONETIC) AT THE

22   UPS STORE. AND --

23   THE COURT: "DEAR TED, PLEASE ACCEPT OUR APOLOGIES.

24   AGAIN, I CAN UNDERSTAND HOW" -- "THANK YOU FOR SENDING US THE

25   PHOTOS. I WILL" -- OKAY, SO THIS IS THE UPS STORE PEOPLE,

26   RIGHT? AND THEY HAVE NO AUTHORITY WHATSOEVER, THESE PEOPLE

27   YOU'RE --

28   MR. CHELDIN: ZERO, ZERO.

1   THE COURT: OKAY.

2   MR. CHELDIN: THEY'RE THE -- THEY'RE CONSIDERED THE

3   SHIPPER, ACTUALLY.

4   THE COURT: OKAY. ALL RIGHT. AND THEN I HAVE WHAT

5   LOOKS LIKE A LETTER OR SOME SORT OF MEMO WITH THE UPS LOGO AT

6   THE TOP, AND IT SAYS, "ATTENTION: PATRICK POWERS" (PHONETIC).

7   MR. CHELDIN: YEAH. I THINK HE'S THE OWNER OF THE

8   STORE.

9   THE COURT: WHAT'S HE SENDING TO YOUR --

10   MR. CHELDIN: IT'S THE -- IT'S A DENIAL. THIS IS --

11 THE LAST THING BEFORE ALL THE PICTURES IS THE DENIAL. IT'S A

12 COUPLE PAGES, WHERE THEY DENIED IT BASED ON --

13   THE COURT: "NEW SINGLE-WALL, CORRUGATED SHIPPING

14   CONTAINER WITH NO VISIBLE BOTTOM MOUNT WAS NOT

15   SUFFICIENT TO PROTECT THE MERCHANDISE. THE USE OF

16   LESS THAN TWO INCHES OF CUSHIONING DID NOT

17   ADEQUATELY PROTECT THE MERCHANDISE. THE MERCHANDISE

18   WAS NOT PROPERLY PLACED".

19   OKAY, SO HOW DO YOU -- HOW DO YOU ADDRESS THESE

20 CLAIMS THAT ACTUALLY, IT'S NOT THEIR -- I CAN'T ENTER JUDGMENT

21 AGAINST THEM IF THEY WEREN'T RESPONSIBLE FOR THE DAMAGE.

22 THEY'RE SAYING IT'S ACTUALLY YOUR FAULT, MR. CHELDIN.

23   MR. CHELDIN: EXACTLY. THEY'RE WANTING -- THEY'RE

24 WANTING THE CUSTOMERS TO BURDEN AND SHOULDER THE UNFORESEEN

25 EVENT OF IMPROPER PACKAGING. IT WAS IMPLIED THAT IT WAS

26 PROPERLY PACKAGED BECAUSE THEY DON'T TURN ANYTHING AWAY. THEY

27 ACCEPT IT. IT COULD HAVE BEEN WRAPPED IN TISSUE PAPER IF THEY

28 ACCEPT -- OR BADLY WRAPPED AND JIGGLING AND RATTLING. IF THEY

1 ACCEPTED IT, AND IT GOT CRUSHED, WHICH IT PROBABLY WOULD IF
2 IT'S RATTLING IN SHABBY --
3   THE COURT: SO WHAT YOU'RE SAYING IS THAT THEIR
4 BUSINESS PRACTICES ARE SUCH THAT THEY'RE NOT LIKE THE POSTAL
5 SERVICE, WHICH WILL ACTUALLY TELL YOU THAT THIS IS NOT GOING
6 TO --
7   MR. CHELDIN: THEY DON'T SEND ANYTHING AWAY. THEY
8 CAN'T -- IT'S A -- IT'S A FALLACY, YOUR -- IT'S A -- IT'S A --
9 THE CONVERSE OF A FALLACY. THEY CAN'T HAVE IT BOTH WAYS.
10 IT'S EITHER SIMULTANEOUSLY TRUE OR SIMULTANEOUSLY -- YOU HAVE
11 TO SEND EVERYTHING AWAY, OR YOU HAVE TO ACCEPT EVERYTHING.
12 AND BOTH -- BOTH CONDITIONS DON'T EXIST AT THE SAME TIME.
13 BECAUSE THEY'RE ACCEPTING -- THEY'RE ACCEPTING EVERYTHING SO
14 LATER DOWN THE ROAD, THEY COULD WIGGLE OUT OF A CLAIM WHEN
15 THEIR DRIVER RUNS IT OVER AND CRUSHES IT AND DESTROYS IT.
16 IT'S -- IT'S ILL-GOTTEN GAINS. IT'S -- IT'S A SCHEME.
17 I'VE -- WHEN WE GET TO EXHIBIT 3, I'M NOT -- THIS IS NOT A
18 UNIQUE SITUATION.
19   THE COURT: OKAY.
20   MR. CHELDIN: A SUFFICIENT CONDITION, YOUR HONOR, IF
21 I COULD JUST STRESS THIS POINT --
22   THE COURT: YEAH, YEAH.
23   MR. CHELDIN: -- EXISTS WHEN A CUSTOMER BRINGS IN
24 THE PACKAGE. THEY'RE -- THEY'RE HAVING A NECESSARY CONDITION
25 EXIST AS WELL, AFTER IT'S INFERRED AT THAT POINT THAT THERE'S
26 AN OFFER AND ACCEPTANCE. THERE'S A BREACH OF CONTRACT.
27 THAT'S A BREACH OF AN IMPLIED COVENANT OF GOOD FAITH AND FAIR
28 DEALING.

1   THAT'S -- LOOK, I'M NOT A LAWYER. I DIDN'T GO TO

2   LAW -- I THINK IT'S OBJECTIVE DOCTRINE THEORY. WHY -- WHAT

3   WOULD -- WHAT'S THE PURPOSE OF BRINGING SOMETHING IN THERE AND

4   HAVING THEM SHIP IT IF THEIR DRIVER, IN THEIR CARE AND

5   CUSTODY, DESTROYS IT? THAT'S THE -- WHERE THE FRAUD COMES IN.

6   THAT'S A MATERIAL MISREPRESENTATION, WHEN THEY'RE KNOWINGLY

7   DOING THIS --

8   THE COURT: YEAH.

9   MR. CHELDIN: -- CONTINUALLY. AND --

10   THE COURT: OKAY. OKAY.

11   MR. CHELDIN: -- DENYING CLAIM --

12   THE COURT: HANG ON, HANG ON, HANG ON. BUT HERE'S

13   THE -- OKAY, HERE'S THE PROBLEM, ALL RIGHT? YOU'VE GOT TO

14   SHOW THAT THIS IS SOMEHOW -- YOU'RE SUING UPS, ALL RIGHT?

15   YOU'VE GOT TO SHOW THAT THE PEOPLE AT THAT SHOP ARE UNDER A --

16   SEE, THIS IS THE DIFFICULTY OF THIS. YOU'VE GOT TO SHOW THAT

17   THE PEOPLE AT THAT SHOP ARE UNDER SOME SORT OF BUSINESS POLICY

18   THAT -- YOU UNDERSTAND, THAT YOU -- EVERYTHING THAT YOU'VE

19   JUST DESCRIBED HAS TO BE PART OF SOME HIDDEN MEMORANDUM

20   SOMEWHERE IN THE FILES OF UPS THAT ALL OF THE WORKERS OF UPS

21   ARE GOING TO -- ARE GOING TO JUST BASICALLY ACCEPT EVERYTHING

22   REGARDLESS. AND THEIR INDEPENDENT REVIEW DEPARTMENT IS JUST

23   GOING TO DENY -- YOU UNDERSTAND WHAT I'M SAYING? YOU'VE GOT

24   TO SHOW IT'S NOT JUST -- IT'S NOT JUST THESE PARTICULAR

25   INDIVIDUALS AT THIS PARTICULAR STORE. YOU'VE GOT TO SHOW THAT

26   IT'S A CORPORATE-WIDE POLICY.

27   MR. CHELDIN: YOUR HONOR, IT IS A PATTERN IN

28   PRACTICE. IT'S BEEN GOING ON -- IT'S -- IT'S --

```
 1              THE COURT:  OKAY.  IS THAT WHAT EXHIBIT 3 IS GOING
 2    TO SHOW ME?
 3              MR. CHELDIN:  EXACTLY, YOUR HONOR.  IT'S BEEN GOING
 4    ON -- I -- THERE'S THOUSANDS -- IF YOU WANT TO TAKE A FIVE-
 5    MINUTE RECESS AND GOOGLE IT YOURSELF AND SEE THE COMPLAINTS ON
 6    DIFFERENT FORUMS -- I DIDN'T WANT TO BOTHER THE COURT WITH A
 7    MOUNTAIN OF COMPLAINTS.  SO I TOOK 3 GOING OVER THE PAST 13
 8    YEARS.  IF YOU WANT TO MOVE FORWARD TO -- TO --
 9              THE COURT:  ALL RIGHT.  I'M GOING TO GO TO EXHIBIT
10    3.
11              MR. CHELDIN:  -- NUMBER 3.  THE FIRST ONE --
12              THE COURT:  ALL RIGHT.  IT SAYS, "BETTER BUSINESS
13    BUREAU".  THERE'S SOME SORT OF --
14              MR. CHELDIN:  THERE'S THE -- THERE'S WHERE --
15              THE COURT:  THERE'S SOME SORT OF WEBPAGE.  YOU'VE
16    COPIED SOME SORT OF WEBPAGE, OR --
17              MR. CHELDIN:  YEAH.  IT'S --
18              THE COURT:  -- IS THIS AN EMAIL?
19              MR. CHELDIN:  THE -- THE FORUMS ARE BASICALLY THE --
20    THE COMPLAINT FORUMS.
21              THE COURT:  OKAY.  SO IT SAYS, "GUARANTEE, GUARANTEE
22    ISSUES.  STATUS:  ANSWERED.  AUGUST 3RD, 2020".
23              MR. CHELDIN:  ALL THESE ARE FOR INSUFFICIENT --
24    THESE ARE COMPLAINTS ABOUT INSUFFICIENT PACKAGING.  THIS ONE
25    IS TWO YEARS AGO.
26              THE COURT:  RIGHT.
27              "I SHIPPED A POOL PACKAGE BY THE MANUFACTURER.  UPS
28              LOST IT FOR TWO TO THREE WEEKS, THEN RETURNED IT
```

1   DESTROYED. THEY THEN DENIED MY INSURANCE CLAIM. I
2   SHIPPED A PACKAGE WITH THE ABOVE TRACKING NUMBER.
3   UPS LOSE" OR THEY MEANT TO SAY, LOST "THE PACKAGE
4   FOR OVER TWO WEEKS, FINALLY FOUND IT AND RETURNED IT
5   TO ME."
6   MR. CHELDIN: IF YOU TURN --
7   THE COURT: "TOTALLY NEW OUTSIDE BOX BECAUSE THEY
8   HAD COMPLETELY DESTROYED THE ORIGINAL ONE. I FILED
9   AN INSURANCE CLAIM WITH THEM TO RECOVER WHAT I AM
10   ENTITLED TO UNDER INSURANCE. THEY DENIED IT, SAYING
11   THE POOL WAS NOT PACKAGED PROPERLY. THIS WAS BASED
12   ON A PHONY" -- "PHONE INTERVIEW" -- EXCUSE ME --
13   "AFTER THEY FAILED TO SHOW UP FOR THE IN-PERSON
14   INTERVIEW FOR ALMOST A WEEK. THE ITEM WAS A BESTWAY
15   POOL" -- OKAY, ET CETERA.
16   ALL RIGHT. LET'S --
17   MR. CHELDIN: THE SECOND --
18   THE COURT: -- MOVE ON TO THE NEXT ONE.
19   MR. CHELDIN: THE SECOND PAGE IS --
20   THE COURT: "HAS UPS EVER PAID A DAMAGE CLAIM?"
21   MR. CHELDIN: THIS IS AN EBAY -- THE EBAY FORUM, THE
22   EBAY COMMUNITY IN 2013, GOING -- WHAT IS THAT -- NINE YEARS
23   AGO. THE SECOND --
24   THE COURT: IT SAYS 2013. IT SAYS OCTOBER 2ND,
25   2013.
26   "I SHIP A FAIR AMOUNT OF PACKAGES EVERY MONTH.
27   THEY'VE DONE A GREAT JOB AND DAMAGED VERY FEW
28   PACKAGES. BUT HERE'S THE BUT: THEY'VE NEVER PAID

1   ANY CLAIMS TO US. THEY ALWAYS FIND SOME REASON OUR
2   PACKING DID NOT MEET SPECIFICATIONS."
3   MR. CHELDIN: THERE YOU GO. AND THAT -- AND THE --
4 THE -- AFTER THE --
5   THE COURT: OKAY. SO BASICALLY, I'M GOING TO HAVE
6 TO REINTERPRET YOUR ARGUMENT, SIR. BECAUSE YOUR ARGUMENT
7 IS -- THE LOSER ARGUMENT YOU HAVE IS THAT IN TAKING IN ITEMS,
8 THERE'S SOME SORT OF CORPORATE POLICY ABOUT JUST BASICALLY NOT
9 PAYING ATTENTION. I THINK YOUR ARGUMENT REALLY -- THE
10 STRONGER ARGUMENT YOU HAVE IS THAT THE CLAIMS DEPARTMENT THAT
11 LOOKS AT THESE THINGS HAS A CORPORATE POLICY OF NEVER PAYING
12 FOR THEM. I THINK -- DO YOU UNDERSTAND WHAT I'M SAYING?
13 BECAUSE I THINK IT'D --
14   MR. CHELDIN: WELL, YOUR HONOR --
15   THE COURT: -- BE VERY DIFFICULT FOR YOU -- IT'D BE
16 VERY DIFFICULT, I THINK, FOR YOU TO SHOW THAT ALL OF THE UPS
17 INDIVIDUAL FRANCHISEES OR WHOEVER THEY ARE, RIGHT, THAT
18 THERE'S A CORPORATE MEMO THAT GOES OUT THAT SAYS, JUST TAKE
19 EVERYTHING IN --
20   MR. CHELDIN: WELL --
21   THE COURT: -- AND JUST --
22   MR. CHELDIN: -- YEAH, I KNOW. THAT'S BECAUSE WE'RE
23 IN SMALL CLAIMS COURT, AND I HAVE STREET KNOWLEDGE, AND I READ
24 A LOT. THAT'S HOW I'M PIECING THIS TOGETHER. I HOPE --
25   THE COURT: I UNDERSTAND, BUT --
26   MR. CHELDIN: -- THAT --
27   THE COURT: -- I CAN ONLY DECIDE BY THE EVIDENCE
28 THAT'S IN FRONT OF ME. I MEAN, I CAN --

1　　　　　MR. CHELDIN:　I -- I KNOW.

2　　　　　THE COURT:　-- DO SOME RESEARCH AS A SMALL CLAIMS

3　JUDGE.　I CAN, BUT -- OKAY.

4　　　　　MR. CHELDIN:　I WOULD -- I WOULD, YOU KNOW, HOPE

5　THAT THE COURT WILL FILL IN THE LEGAL GAPS --

6　　　　　THE COURT:　WELL, BUT I --

7　　　　　MR. CHELDIN:　-- OF THE --

8　　　　　THE COURT:　YOU KNOW, IT'S NOT MY JOB TO BE

9　SPECULATIVE, OKAY?　IT'S MY JOB TO ACTUALLY DRAW WHATEVER

10　INFERENCES I CAN DRAW FROM THE EVIDENCE THAT I HAVE, ALL

11　RIGHT?

12　　　　　MR. CHELDIN:　UNDERSTOOD.

13　　　　　THE COURT:　YOU'RE ASKING ME TO BASICALLY -- YOU'RE

14　ASKING ME TO DEVELOP A THEORY ABOUT THIS, AND I WOULD RATHER

15　JUST ACT DEDUCTIVELY, NOT INDUCTIVELY, AND TRY TO, YOU KNOW,

16　ARRIVE AT SOME SORT OF -- SOME SORT OF THEORY OF HOW UPS

17　WORKS.　THAT'S REALLY THE JOB OF A PROSECUTING ATTORNEY OR A

18　PLAINTIFF'S ATTORNEY TO DRAW THAT.　I HAVE TO TRY TO GET WHAT

19　I CAN FROM THE EVIDENCE THAT YOU'VE GIVEN ME.　ALL RIGHT.

20　SO --

21　　　　　MR. CHELDIN:　UNDERSTOOD, YOUR HONOR.

22　　　　　THE COURT:　OKAY.　"HAS UPS EVER PAID A DAMAGE

23　CLAIM?"　AND IT SAYS -- THIS IS ALSO FROM OCTOBER 3RD.　SO IT

24　SAYS THERE, "IT'S LIKELY THEY'RE PLANNING AHEAD TO DENY CLAIMS

25　BASED ON INSUFFICIENT PACKAGING."　OKAY.　SO THAT SEEMS TO

26　BE -- THERE SEEMS TO BE AT LEAST AN INTERNET MEME --

27　　　　　MR. CHELDIN:　YES.

28　　　　　THE COURT:　-- THAT EVERYBODY SAYS, LOOK, WHEN

1 YOU'RE DENIED, IT'S ALWAYS BECAUSE YOU DIDN'T --

2   MR. CHELDIN: WELL, IT'S -- IT'S --

3   THE COURT: -- SUFFICIENTLY PACKAGE.

4   MR. CHELDIN: -- MORE THAN THAT. THERE'S THOUSANDS,

5 LIKE I SAID. AND THE LAST ONE IS FROM RIG-TALK. I THINK IT'S

6 A GUITAR MUSIC -- I THINK IT'S A --

7   THE COURT: YEAH, IT SAYS, "SHIPPED MESA, DECEMBER

8 30, 2010."

9   MR. CHELDIN: THAT'S 12 YEARS AGO. IN THE FIRST

10 PARAGRAPH THERE.

11   THE COURT: YEAH, I SEE IT. IT SAYS, "UPS DENIED

12 CLAIM" --

13   MR. CHELDIN: PACKAGING WAS NOT SUFFICIENT.

14   THE COURT: -- "SAYING THAT PACKAGING WAS NOT

15 SUFFICIENT."

16   MR. CHELDIN: YEAH, THAT'S -- THAT'S PRETTY MUCH --

17 YOU KNOW. THE -- I JUST PUT THE REST OF IT IN BECAUSE THAT

18 WAS THE THREAD ON THAT.

19   THE COURT: OKAY. AND THEN THERE'S ANOTHER ONE.

20 "YEP, THAT'S THE RUBBER STAMP DENIAL THEY THROW OUT EVERY

21 TIME. THEY ALWAYS CLAIM THE SINGLE-WALL BOX WAS

22 INSUFFICIENT." OKAY.

23   MR. CHELDIN: IT'S -- IT'S VERY MISLEADING --

24   THE COURT: OKAY.

25   MR. CHELDIN: -- CORPORATE -- CORPORATE-WISE. YOU

26 KNOW, IT'S -- IT -- THE COMPENSATORY -- I DON'T SEE HOW THEY

27 ESCAPE NOT PAYING THE CLAIM --

28   THE COURT: OKAY.

1   MR. CHELDIN: -- ON A COMPENSATORY DAMAGE.

2   THE COURT: OKAY. SO LET'S GET NOW -- LET'S GET

3   NOW -- THEY'VE ALREADY -- I MEAN, BASICALLY, THE DEFENDANT HAS

4   ALREADY ADMITTED AT LEAST LIABILITY OF $217.75. LET'S GET TO

5   ALL THESE OTHER STUFF. I'M JUST NOT SURE --

6   MR. CHELDIN: YOUR --

7   THE COURT: EXPLAIN TO ME HOW YOU ARRIVED AT THE

8   EXEMPLARY DAMAGES. BECAUSE THAT'S ALL THAT'S REALLY LEFT. OR

9   ARE THERE ANY INCIDENTAL OR CONSEQUENTIAL DAMAGES THAT ARE NOT

10   IN THE 217.75?

11   MR. CHELDIN: PRE-COURT INTEREST. YOU KNOW, IT'S

12   BEEN A YEAR, YOU KNOW, FOR 10 PERCENT.

13   THE COURT: OKAY, SO 10 PERCENT ON 217.75?

14   MR. CHELDIN: SURE.

15   THE COURT: ALL RIGHT. WE'LL ADD THAT.

16   MR. CHELDIN: YOUR --

17   THE COURT: SO THAT WOULD BE WHAT? THAT WOULD BE

18   $22? $21.70? NO?

19   MR. CHELDIN: YES, YOUR HONOR.

20   THE COURT: HANG ON. LET ME JUST DO THAT. LET ME

21   JUST --

22   MR. CHELDIN: APPROXIMATELY $20.

23   THE COURT: EQUALS $21.76. OKAY. SO LET'S TAKE

24   THAT INTEREST. WHAT ELSE? WHAT OTHER CONSEQUENTIAL OR

25   INCIDENTAL DAMAGES?

26   MR. CHELDIN: THE --

27   THE COURT: AND I'M NOT GETTING TO EXEMPLARY YET.

28   I'M JUST GETTING TO WHAT REALLY --

1   MR. CHELDIN: OKAY, YOUR HONOR.

2   THE COURT: -- FROM -- OKAY.

3   MR. CHELDIN: THERE WAS $15 AND -- I DON'T KNOW.

4 ANOTHER -- THESE ARE COURT COSTS FOR THE EVIDENCE.

5   THE COURT: WELL, I'LL GET YOU THAT AT THE END IF

6 YOU WIN.

7   MR. CHELDIN: OKAY.

8   THE COURT: OKAY.

9   MR. CHELDIN: PHOTOCOPIES, $8.60. IT WAS A LOT MORE

10 THAN -- THAT'S FOR ALL THE EVIDENCE. THERE WAS A LOT MORE,

11 BUT I ONLY HAVE RECEIPTS FOR 8 -- I COULDN'T --

12   THE COURT: OKAY. ALL RIGHT, ALL RIGHT. SO --

13   MR. CHELDIN: -- COULDN'T FIND MY --

14   THE COURT: -- WE NEED TO DO THAT.

15   MR. CHELDIN: SO 8 -- 8.60 --

16   THE COURT: HANG ON, HANG ON, HANG ON. OKAY, SO

17 I'VE GOT 217.75 PLUS 21.76 PLUS $8.60. AND THIS IS WHAT

18 YOU'RE TELLING ME UNDER PENALTY OF PERJURY, CORRECT?

19   MR. CHELDIN: CORRECT.

20   THE COURT: BECAUSE I DON'T SEE A RECEIPT HERE FOR

21 ANY OF THIS. BUT OKAY.

22   MR. CHELDIN: CORRECT.

23   THE COURT: SO I'VE GOT $248.11. NOW, HOW DO I --

24 HOW DO I GET TO $4,700 FROM THERE? WHAT KIND OF -- I MEAN,

25 YOU'RE ASKING FOR A TON OF EXEMPLARY DAMAGES, EMOTIONAL

26 DISTRESS. I MEAN, THE EMOTIONAL DISTRESS, YOU'D HAVE TO SHOW

27 ME THAT SOMEHOW YOU HAD TO GO SEE A PSYCHIATRIST OR SOMETHING,

28 YOU HAD TO GET MEDICATIONS, YOUR LIFE WAS -- YOUR DAY-TO-DAY

1 LIFE WAS CHANGED BY ALL THIS. I'M LOOKING AT YOU RIGHT NOW.

2 YOU'RE ARGUING VERY COGENTLY, SO I DON'T THINK THAT YOUR LIFE

3 FUNCTIONS HAVE BEEN DRAMATICALLY CHANGED BY THIS.

4   MR. CHELDIN: YOUR HONOR --

5   THE COURT: SO HOW DO I GET TO $4,700?

6   MR. CHELDIN: -- I COMPLETELY UNDERSTAND. I ASKED

7 FOR A NOMINAL AMOUNT, I FEEL. IF YOU FEEL I HAVE PROVEN MY

8 CASE, PLEASE FEEL YOUR DISCRETION TO ADJUST THEM UP OR --

9   THE COURT: OKAY. BUT WHAT I -- I DON'T MIND USING

10 A MULTIPLIER, BUT I HAVE TO USE THIS AS A BASIS, $248.11.

11 OKAY?

12   MR. CHELDIN: I USED FIVE. IF YOU WANT TO DO A TWO,

13 I WOULD LIKE A -- I WOULD LIKE TO KNOW THAT THE JOURNEY OF

14 1,000 MILES BEGINS WITH THIS FIRST STEP.

15   THE COURT: OKAY. I GET IT. ALL RIGHT. I GET IT.

16 I --

17   MR. CHELDIN: THIS NEEDS TO -- THEY CAN'T CONTINUE

18 LIKE THIS, SO MORE PEOPLE, HOPEFULLY, WILL COME IF WE HAVE

19 SOME VINDICATION, YOU KNOW, HERE --

20   THE COURT: WELL, THEN --

21   MR. CHELDIN: -- THAT THIS IS -- THIS IS ACTUALLY

22 WHAT'S HAPPENING.

23   THE COURT: OKAY. WELL, THEN WHAT NEEDS TO HAPPEN

24 IS A CLASS ACTION AT SOME POINT. AND I'M JUST LOOKING --

25   MR. CHELDIN: WE'RE BARRED. THAT'S THE PROBLEM.

26 THE SUPERIOR BARGAINING POWER FROM THE CONTRACT HAS BARRED

27 ANYONE FROM CLASS -- I SPOKE TO TIM FISHER UP IN NORTHERN

28 CALIFORNIA. HE'S A CLASS -- I HAVE HIS PHONE NUMBER HERE. I

1 SPOKE TO DAVID DORNFELD (PHONETIC), WHO TURNED ME ON TO TIM
2 FISHER. HE SAID, WE BELIEVE THERE'S A PATTERN IN PRACTICE,
3 AND THEY'RE -- THEY'RE A BUNCH OF CROOKS, AND WE CAN'T GET
4 AROUND THIS ARBITRATION CLAUSE FOR THE CLASS ACTION. IT
5 ALSO -- I CAN'T DO A -- (INDISCERNIBLE).
6   THE COURT: OKAY. LET ME ASK YOU SOMETHING. WHAT
7 WAS THE -- ALSO, YOU'RE FORGETTING SOMETHING. WHAT WAS THE
8 VALUE OF THE ARTWORK?
9   MR. CHELDIN: THE VALUE WAS $225 ORIGINALLY, AND IT
10 WAS REDUCED TO SELL TO $170. BUT THIS IS LIKE A STATE --
11   THE COURT: NO, NO, I JUST NEED -- OKAY, I'M
12 TRYING --
13   MR. CHELDIN: $200. OKAY, I'M SORRY, YOUR HONOR.
14   THE COURT: I'M TRYING TO GET --
15   MR. CHELDIN: I DIDN'T --
16   THE COURT: -- WHAT ARE THE INCIDENTALS IN --
17   MR. CHELDIN: SURE.
18   THE COURT: YOU UNDERSTAND?
19   MR. CHELDIN: $200.
20   THE COURT: WHAT IS THE -- BECAUSE NOW, THAT LADY
21 CAN'T KEEP IT. YOU HAD TO PROBABLY RETURN HER MONEY, RIGHT?
22   MR. CHELDIN: I DID, RIGHT AWAY.
23   THE COURT: OKAY, SO WHAT WAS THAT?
24   MR. CHELDIN: $200, YOUR HONOR.
25   THE COURT: IT WAS $200?
26   MR. CHELDIN: YES.
27   THE COURT: OKAY, SO I ADD $200. $448. OKAY. ALL
28 RIGHT.

1   MR. CHELDIN: THE -- THE EXEMPLARY DAMAGE --

2   THE COURT: OKAY, HANG ON.

3   MR. CHELDIN: OH.

4   THE COURT: I'M GETTING THERE. OKAY. I'M GETTING

5 THERE. ALL RIGHT. SO I THINK A GOOD MULTIPLIER MAYBE IS BY

6 THREE. SO I MULTIPLY THIS BY THREE.

7   MR. CHELDIN: I UNDERSTAND, YOUR HONOR.

8   THE COURT: OKAY. ALL RIGHT.

9   MR. CHELDIN: AND I -- I AGREE WITH YOU.

10   THE COURT: OKAY. ALL RIGHT. SO LET ME GO TO THE

11 DEFENDANT NOW, AND YOU'LL HAVE THE LAST WORD.

12   MR. CHELDIN: THANK YOU, YOUR HONOR.

13   THE COURT: BECAUSE IT'S ALWAYS PLAINTIFF,

14 DEFENDANT, PLAINTIFF.

15   MR. CHELDIN: THANK YOU, YOUR HONOR.

16   THE COURT: ALL RIGHT. SIR, REPRESENTATIVE FOR

17 UNITED PARCEL, YOU'VE BEEN HEARING WHAT I'VE BEEN SAYING IN

18 ALL THIS. YOU'VE ADMITTED ALREADY THAT YOUR COMPANY'S WILLING

19 TO PAY THE $217.75. DO YOU HAVE ANY EVIDENCE WITH RESPECT TO

20 THE ARGUMENT THAT ESSENTIALLY YOUR COMPANY IS IN BAD FAITH, IS

21 VIOLATING THE COVENANT OF GOOD FAITH AND FAIR DEALING, AND IT

22 ALREADY KNOWS AHEAD OF TIME THAT IT'S NOT GOING TO PAY FOR ANY

23 DAMAGES TO THE PROPERTY? DO YOU HAVE ANY EVIDENCE -- DO YOU

24 HAVE ANY TESTIMONY IN THAT REGARD?

25   MR. AVITIA: WELL, I CAN ONLY SPEAK FOR MYSELF,

26 AND --

27   THE COURT: WELL, YOU CAN'T SPEAK FOR YOURSELF.

28   MR. AVITIA: -- THE CLAIMS THAT I SEE --

1   THE COURT: SIR, LISTEN. YOU CAN'T SPEAK FOR
2   YOURSELF. YOU HAVE TO SPEAK FOR THE COMPANY, OKAY?
3   MR. AVITIA: OKAY.
4   THE COURT: SO --
5   MR. AVITIA: WELL, I'LL SPEAK FROM THE POSITION THAT
6   I AM IN THE COMPANY AND THE CLAIMS THAT I'VE SEEN GONE
7   THROUGH. WE HAVE PAID CLAIMS IN THE PAST, AND I WISH TO
8   REFERENCE A SECTION OF THE TERMS AND CONDITIONS IN REGARDS TO
9   THE CONSEQUENTIAL DAMAGES, IF I MAY.
10   THE COURT: OKAY. THAT WOULD BE HIS EXHIBIT 1.
11 OKAY. GO AHEAD. TELL ME.
12   MR. AVITIA: YEAH. IT'S GOING TO BE ON THE -- I
13 THINK IT'S THE SIXTH PARAGRAPH. "ANY STATEMENT BIAS REGARDING
14 A PROBABLE" --
15   THE COURT: "DATE AND" --
16   MR. AVITIA: -- "DATE AND, IF APPLICABLE, TIME OF
17 DELIVERY IS ONLY AN ESTIMATE AND IS NOT WARRANTED IN ANY
18 MANNER."
19   THE COURT: ALL RIGHT. OKAY, BUT LET'S --
20   MR. AVITIA: (INDISCERNIBLE).
21   THE COURT: -- AND LET ME STOP YOU. LET ME STOP
22 YOU. LET ME STOP YOU. LET ME STOP YOU. THAT PARAGRAPH IS
23 ABOUT TIMELY DELIVERY. IT'S NOT ABOUT -- OKAY, I'LL READ THE
24 WHOLE PARAGRAPH. I ALREADY READ IT WHEN I WAS GOING THROUGH
25 THE PLAINTIFF'S EVIDENCE.
26   "WE ARE NOT LIABLE FOR ANY CONSEQUENTIAL, INDIRECT,
27   SPECIAL, INCIDENTAL, OR PUNITIVE DAMAGES OR ANY LOSS
28   OR DAMAGE RESULTING FROM DELAYS IN SHIPPING OR

1   DELIVERY".

2   DELAYS. IT'S NOT ABOUT -- "OUR RESPONSIBILITY FOR

3 DAMAGE TO ITEMS CAUSED BY" -- OKAY, HANG ON. YOU GOT IT.

4 FORGIVE ME. IT'S THE THIRD SENTENCE.

5   "OUR RESPONSIBILITY FOR DAMAGE TO ITEMS CAUSED BY

6   IMPROPER PACKING BY US IS LIMITED TO ANY APPLIED

7   DECLARED VALUE PROGRAM OR OTHER PROGRAM THAT WE MAY

8   OFFER FOR WHICH YOU HAVE PAID ANY APPLICABLE

9   CHARGE."

10   OKAY. SO GIVEN THAT, LET'S SAY, OKAY, YOU'RE

11 LIMITED TO THE $200. OKAY, CAN YOU GIVE ME SOME KIND OF

12 EVIDENCE THAT YOU DON'T ALWAYS JUST TAKE EVERYTHING THAT --

13 YOU KNOW, JUST BASICALLY DECLARE THAT EVERYTHING IS SIMPLY

14 IMPROPERLY PACKAGED?

15   MR. AVITIA: I -- I DON'T HAVE ANY EVIDENCE FOR

16 THAT. I --

17   THE COURT: OKAY.

18   MR. AVITIA: -- I DO NOT WORK IN THE CLAIMS

19 DEPARTMENT.

20   THE COURT: YEAH, RIGHT. OKAY. ALL RIGHT. IS

21 THERE ANYTHING ELSE YOU WANT TO TELL ME? YOU KNOW, I DON'T

22 HAVE ANY EVIDENCE FROM YOU OTHER THAN THE CONTRACT HERE. IS

23 THERE ANYTHING ELSE YOU WANT TO TELL ME?

24   MR. AVITIA: NO. THAT WILL BE ALL, YOUR HONOR.

25   THE COURT: OKAY. I'LL GIVE YOU THE LAST WORD, SIR.

26 BUT YOU CAN MAKE IT BRIEF, PLEASE.

27   MR. CHELDIN: YES, YOUR HONOR. YOU UNDERSTAND. I

28 DON'T NEED TO WASTE ANY MORE OF THE COURT'S VALUABLE TIME.

1 YOU -- I FEEL YOU'RE A VERY CONSCIENTIOUS JUDGE, AND YOU

2 UNDERSTAND THE SITUATION. I FEEL I'VE PROVEN THE CASE, AND

3 IT'S REALLY UP TO THE AMOUNTS, REALLY, THAT THE COURT WOULD

4 SEEM JUST AND APPROPRIATE TO --

5   THE COURT: OKAY.

6   MR. CHELDIN: THANK YOU, YOUR HONOR.

7   THE COURT: ALL RIGHT. SO I'VE RECEIVED EVIDENCE

8 THAT ESSENTIALLY, DESPITE THIS CLAUSE IN THE CONTRACT, THAT

9 UPS HAS -- I'VE BEEN GIVEN EVIDENCE THAT UPS SEEMS TO HAVE A

10 CUSTOM AND PRACTICE OF ESSENTIALLY DENYING ALL CLAIMS

11 REGARDLESS. IN THIS INSTANCE, THE PLAINTIFF WAS ACTUALLY

12 FORCED TO SUE UPS JUST TO GET THE DECLARED VALUE OF THE ITEM.

13 AND I'VE RECEIVED EVIDENCE THAT THE DECLARED VALUE WAS $200.

14   YOU KNOW WHAT? I'M SORRY. I DOUBLED THAT WHEN I

15 SHOULD NOT HAVE. OKAY, I ADDED AN ADDITIONAL $200 WHEN IN

16 FACT --

17   MR. CHELDIN: I THOUGHT -- I THOUGHT THAT WAS FOR

18 THE EMOTIONAL.

19   THE COURT: YEAH.

20   MR. CHELDIN: OKAY.

21   THE COURT: OKAY.

22   MR. CHELDIN: THAT'S FINE, YOUR HONOR.

23   THE COURT: I'M SORRY, I DID THAT. I ADDED AN

24 ADDITIONAL $200 WHEN I SHOULDN'T HAVE DONE THAT.

25   MR. CHELDIN: YEAH.

26   THE COURT: 217. SO BASICALLY, IF I TAKE $248.11

27 TIMES 3 -- I THINK A MULTIPLIER OF 3 IS SUFFICIENT --

28   MR. CHELDIN: YES.

1   THE COURT: -- IN THIS INSTANCE --

2   MR. CHELDIN: YES. YOU SAID THAT.

3   THE COURT: -- I GET $744.33. CAN WE JUST MAKE IT

4 744?

5   MR. CHELDIN: YES, YOUR HONOR.

6   THE COURT: OKAY. ALL RIGHT, SO I'M GOING TO ENTER

7 PRINCIPAL JUDGMENT IN FAVOR OF THE PLAINTIFF IN THE SUM OF

8 $744. OKAY, WHAT WERE YOUR COURT COSTS, SIR?

9   THE CLERK: $90.

10   THE COURT: IS THAT CORRECT, SIR, $90?

11   MR. CHELDIN: I HAD ANOTHER $30.10 FOR THE EVIDENCE

12 THAT WAS SUBMITTED TO THE -- 15.05 FOR THE COURT AND 15.05 FOR

13 THE DEFENDANT.

14   THE COURT: OKAY. ALL RIGHT, SO WE'RE TALKING ABOUT

15 $120 IN COSTS?

16   MR. CHELDIN: YES, SIR.

17   THE COURT: OKAY. SO PRINCIPAL JUDGMENT OF $744

18 PLUS $120 IN COSTS, FOR A TOTAL JUDGMENT OF $864. SO DID YOU

19 GET THAT, JOHN?

20   THE CLERK: I DID.

21   THE COURT: 744 PRINCIPAL, 120 IN COSTS, AND 864

22 TOTAL JUDGMENT. ALL RIGHT. THANK YOU BOTH VERY MUCH.

23   THE CLERK: THE EXHIBITS ARE --

24   THE COURT: AND YOU WANT YOUR EXHIBITS BACK, SIR?

25   MR. CHELDIN: SURE. THANK YOU, YOUR HONOR.

26   THE COURT: HERE YOU GO, DEPUTY.

27   THE JUDICIAL ASSISTANT: ARE THEY ALL PLAINTIFF'S?

28   THE COURT: YEAH, THEY'RE ALL PLAINTIFF'S. I DIDN'T

1 GET ANYTHING FROM --

2   ALL RIGHT. THANK YOU VERY MUCH.

3   MR. CHELDIN: THANK YOU, YOUR HONOR. I APPRECIATE

4 IT.

5   THE COURT: ALL RIGHT. NOW, YOU'RE GOING TO HAVE TO

6 COLLECT IT.

7   MR. CHELDIN: YES, SIR.

8   (PROCEEDINGS CONCLUDED AT 12:01 P.M.)

9   * * * * *

10

11

12

13

14

15

16

17

18

19

20

21

22

23

24

25

26

27

28

1   C E R T I F I C A T E

2   I, COLE TUTINO, TRANSCRIPTIONIST, DO HEREBY CERTIFY

3 THAT THE FOREGOING PAGES, 1 – 35, CONSTITUTE A FULL, TRUE, AND

4 ACCURATE TRANSCRIPT, FROM ELECTRONIC RECORDING, TRANSCRIBED BY

5 ME, OF THE PROCEEDINGS HAD IN THE FOREGOING MATTER, TED

6 CHELDIN V. UNITED PARCEL SERVICE, INC., CASE NO. 22AVSC00096,

7 ON THE DOCKET OF THE SUPERIOR COURT OF THE STATE OF

8 CALIFORNIA, FOR THE COUNTY OF LOS ANGELES, A COURT OF RECORD,

9 AND ALL PREPARED TO THE BEST OF MY SKILL AND ABILITY.

15 _____
COLE TUTINO

16 DIGITAL COURT TRANSCRIBER

17   DATED AND SIGNED THIS 14TH DAY OF JULY, 2022.

Fan Mail

Ted Cheldin
PO Box 2335
Canyon Country, California
91386-2335 USA

Made in the USA
Las Vegas, NV
05 May 2024

89561009R00050